Get **more** out of libraries

Please return or renew this item by the last date shown.
You can renew online at www.hants.gov.uk/library
Or by phoning Hampshire Libraries
Tel: 0300 555 1387

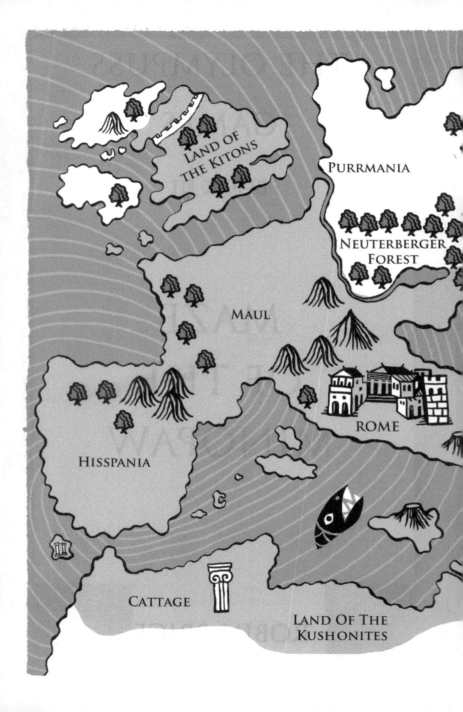

THE OLYMPUSS GAMES
BOOK III: MAZE OF THE MINOPAW

First published by Mogzilla in 2015
Paperback edition:
ISBN: 9781906132828

Printed in the UK

The Olympuss Games

BOOK I Son of Spartapuss   ISBN: 9781906132811

BOOK II Eye of the Cyclaw   ISBN: 9781906132835
BOOK III Maze of the Minopaw ISBN: 9781906132828

BOOK IV Stars of Olympuss   ISBN: 9781906132842

www.mogzilla.co.uk/shop

WWW.SPARTAPUSS.COM

THE STORY SO FAR...

The OLYMPUSS GAMES series is set in ancient Rome where cats rule the world and people have never existed.

The first book in the series is called: SON OF SPARTAPUSS.

The SON OF SPARTAPUSS (or 'S.O.S.' for short) is a young ginger cat from the Land of the Kitons (Britain). He has just moved to Rome with his mother.

At the market he meets FURIA, a mysterious cat with orange eyes. S.O.S. buys FURIA at the auction, but she is far more expensive than he thinks. When S.O.S. can't pay, the seller calls the guards. S.O.S. is fined ten silver coins. An old cat called FATHER FELINIOUS offers to pay the fine if S.O.S. joins his gladiator school: THE SCHOOL FOR STRAYS. When he learns that FELINIOUS is FURIA's new owner, S.O.S. agrees to go. FURIA escapes from the school but gets caught. PUSSPERO MAXI, FURIA and S.O.S. fight their first gladiator battle together. Furia defeats a giant from Cattage.

The second book in the series is called: EYE OF THE CYCLAW.

Excitement spreads around the SCHOOL FOR STRAYS when an official arrives and asks the school to send athletes to MOUNT OLYMPUSS to take part in the famous GAMES.

SON OF SPARTAPUSS is excited. However, qualifying for the games is harder than it looks.

Meanwhile, we learn that the mysterious FURIA is on a quest to recover STRAYBOS (charms that are hidden in different places around the FELINE EMPIRE). One STRAYBO is hidden in the SCHOOL FOR STRAYS. After they find it, MAXI and the SON OF SPARTAPUSS decide to join FURIA on her quest to find the other missing charms. A clue suggests that one charm has been hidden near MOUNT OLYMPUSS, where the GAMES are going to be held. However, to qualify for the games, they must defeat the famous gladiator known as THE CYCLAW.

THE SECRET DIARY OF S.O.S.

MEWNONIUS X

June 10th

Dear mother, I am sorry about the terrible state of this diary. On the way to The Olympuss Games we were shipwrecked. As Squeak islands go, Knossos is not a good place to spend a two week break – unless you like blood sports. King Minos wasn't pleased to see us. He made me fight his top gladiator. Then he locked us all up in an evil maze and I had a nasty run in with a cat-eating monster.

By the way mother, have you got any good tips for getting monster blood off clothes? In case you are wondering how I survived, I have written it all down in this diary.

Your loving son,

S.O.S

P.S. I'm sorry for writing 'scratching post' on your back when we visited the market. I'm a more grown up cat now.

Goodbye To Rome

Finally the great day came – the day when I was going to leave Rome and sail off to take part in the Olympuss games. I can't remember being more excited on any day in my long life – and I am fourteen years old! Father Felinious (the owner of the School for Strays) led the way as we walked along the docks at Ostia.

"Is it that one?" I asked pointing at an enormous ship with black sails.

"That one?" laughed Maxi. "No way! That's a trireme."

"I knew that," I said.

"You've got no idea what a trireme is, have you Spartan?" he asked.

"No," I hissed. "But something tells me you're going to explain EVERYTHING about the Squeaks and their ships."

"Didn't you study sea battles at school?" he laughed. "I expect they don't have schools in Sparta."

I shot Maxi a hard stare.

"I'm not from Sparta," I muttered. "I'm from the Land of the Kitons."

Maxi thinks he knows everything about every subject under the stars. He took a deep breath and started to talk.

"A trireme is a fast warship with three rows of oars arranged in banks of twenty five rowers. It has two masts and a keel made of oak," he began.

"Stars of Andrasta! Spare us the details!" hissed a voice at our side. It was the first thing that Furia had said to us since we left the gladiator school that morning.

Crestfallen, Maxi stopped talking about ships. We passed boat after boat until we came to an ancient looking ship.

"For Peus sake! Not that one!" moaned Maxi. "I've seen shipwrecks in better condition than that!"

Maxi did have a point. Our ship looked as if it had sailed out of the pages of history. Its mast was as crooked as a squirrel's tail. Its sail was the colour of dirty dishwater. On the side I read the ship's name, which had been scratched into the grey wood.

"The Paaaa?" I said. "What sort of name is that for a boat?"

"You ginger half wit! It's not called The Paaa! It's called *The Pawgo*," gushed Maxi in excitement. "It's got the same name as the famous ship used by Sprayson in the old tale."

"Who's he when he's at home?" I sighed.

"Sprayson," said Maxi in a wounded tone. "You know, Sprayson son of Aason. From the famous tale of Sprayson and The Pawgonauts... where they look for The Golden Fleas."

"Aason?" I gasped. "What kind of a stupid name is Aason?"

"Aason is my grandfather's name!" hissed the Captain.

"All aboard!" boomed a voice from the ship. Why do sailors insist on shouting this? Maxi pushed in and sprang up the gangplank ahead of me.

"All aboard!" ordered the voice again.

"Stop saying that! We ARE all aboard," muttered Father Felinious.

"Wait! Where's Wulfren?" asked Maxi.

The Father did not answer. But we soon found out that he had left Wulfren in charge of his gladiator school. So there were only going to be four of us in the Olympuss team: myself, Maxi, Furia and the Father himself.

I admit that I would have felt a lot safer if Wulfren was coming along, (even though our head instructor has a passion for pain).

"Cast off!" called the Father. 'Let's go!"

"What? No wolfy?" moaned Maxi. "Aooowwoooo!" I cried, imitating a wolf.

Furia shot me a dark look and her tail began to flick restlessly. But I think she might have been secretly pleased that we had given Wulfren the slip.

If you read my last scroll, you'll know that Furia had only agreed to come to the games because she was on a quest to find mysterious charms called straybos. She is collecting them and putting them on her collar. I'm not sure why she wants to find them but her grandmother left instructions for her to follow, with clues about where to find the next straybo. I discovered the first one hidden in a training machine in the School for Strays. We are hoping to find the next one somewhere on Mount Olympuss. That's the only reason that Furia is coming to the games. She doesn't want to win for Rome. She hates Rome so much that she refused to fight when Felinious put on a gladiator battle between teams from Rome and Cattage.

Maxi said it was our duty to join her on her quest for these mysterious straybos. But as I stood there on the battered deck, gazing into her fiery amber eyes, I wondered if she needed our help.

Anyway, the captain was a black and white cat called Bustus with torn ears and face markings that made him look as if he was wearing a mask over his yellow eyes. He had matching yellow teeth too.

He padded towards the gangplank with a suspicious look on his mask-like face and fixed the Father with a glare.

"Are you sure about this?" he hissed.

"You've got my silver so I get your ship," said the Father impatiently.

"Take care of her," snapped the captain. "If you don't return her in good order, you'll have to pay for any damages."

And with that, the old sea captain padded slowly away down the gang plank, clutching Father Felinious' bag of silver in his paw.

"Stop!" I called. "Where in Paw's name do you think you're going?"

But old captain Bustus never looked back, he just walked off into the misty morning, counting his silver denari. Who can blame him? I expect he thought that Fortune had spun him a great one there on her wheel. What a great stroke of luck to find a buyer like the Father for a broken down old ship like *The Pawgo*. Eight out of ten cats wouldn't have bought it for firewood.

The Endless Sea

You might be wondering why the Father had dismissed the captain of *The Pawgo* and the crew as well. Well as it turns out he had a good reason, although he wasn't telling us at the time. So I will hold it back from you in order to add a little spice to my story.

As I stood by the docks on that misty morning in Ostia, I was a worried cat. I had never sailed a ship before. And for all of his facts about ships, Maxi didn't know one end of a rope from the other.

I have read quite a lot of books that talk about sea trips. They write about the 'loneliness of the ocean'. The hero is 'crossing the pea-green sea, under the slate grey sky with the endless white-capped waves rolling as far as the eye can see'. Not forgetting 'the haunting call of the seagulls as they float like Neptune's ghosts in the wild winds'.

I don't usually read these bits – I like to skip to the part where the hero's ship gets caught in a terrible storm, as they always do in stories.

The Claws of the Storm

"Help! I can't move!" screamed a worried voice. It was Maxi.

I shook myself awake and sprang from my hammock. At least I tried to spring out of my hammock but I couldn't move. Someone had tied me down.

"Help!" called Maxi again.

"Help! I can't move either!" I cried, joining in.

"Stop copying me, copycat!" he called.

A hammock is the most comfortable bed you can find on a ship. It does not move about when the sea gets rough. That's the idea anyway. But this hammock was shaking like an olive tree in a gale.

I tore at the hammock and tried to escape, but it was no use.

"It's no use," moaned Maxi. "Someone has sewn me into my hammock!"

I could hear him clawing at his hammock, but it was impossible, you'd need claws of iron to tear through the thick canvas.

"What sort of monster would do this?" I asked. "Tying us up like chickens on a pole."

"I would," said a low voice.

"Is that you Father Felinious?" I gasped.

"Why have you sewn us in?" asked Maxi. "Are you worried that we might escape?"

Before he could reply, the boat pitched, rocking our hammocks wildly.

"I sewed you in because I was worried that you might fall off the ship," explained Felinious.

"Why worry about that?" I asked.

"Because you've fallen off three times already," he hissed. "It's a good job that I had Furia to help me drag you back on board."

He was right. It would be hard to find a more useless pair of sailors than Maxi and me.

"Cut us out Father Felinious! For the love of Peus!" I cried.

"Silence!" snapped the Father. "We are in Pawsidon's realm now. He's angry enough as it is."

Sailors are a superstitious bunch and it seemed that Father Felinious was no exception.

I felt the canvas tearing as a long knife

cut away the rope. I tumbled out of the hammock. The boat rocked as it fell off the crest of the wave and crashed into a dip.

"Miaooowch!" I moaned. "That was a big one. It's a wonder that an old ship like this can take all of this punishment. Maybe my father was right? Perhaps they were better at building ships in the old days."

Before these words had left my mouth there was another terrible lurch followed by a grinding sound like giant teeth gnashing. The next thing I knew I was clinging onto the wall with my claws. A fountain of freezing water was spurting into my face.

"Paw's jaws!" I moaned. "What's happening?"

"We're sinking," yelled the Father.

"Sinking?" I moaned. "We're sinking!"

Father Felinious's tail began to flick.

"What in Paws' name do we do now?" I wailed. I didn't want to drown.

"Plug it!!!" snapped Maxi.

"There's no need to be rude," I muttered.

"I mean plug that hole."

When I heard the hiss of the rushing water, I started to panic. I saw a hole in the wall of the ship. It was as wide as a lion's jaws. The icy sea was bursting in and pooling under my shaking paws. A cold fear clawed at me.

We Kitons have a terrible fear of drowning. It is said that if you drown, they won't let you into Summerlands. The Mewids say Summerlands lies 'north of the sky, where the backwards birds fly'. Try finding that on a map! I wasn't sure I really believed in Summerlands, but now was not the time to find out if they were right.

Maxi sprang into action. He grabbed his hammock, rolled it up into a ball and stuffed it into the ragged gap like a cork in a bottle. He pushed against it, putting his full weight behind it. I followed Maxi's example, desperately grabbing blankets and sheets and anything I could lay my paws on to plug up the hole. A few minutes later, it was over. Although the hull was still a bit leaky, we seemed to have got away with it.

"You've done well Spartan!" laughed Maxi.

I like Maxi but I find it kind of annoying when he keeps congratulating me whenever we don't die!

"What should we do now?" I asked.

"Let's get up on deck and find Furia and Felinious." Follow me!" he boomed.

I sprang up the wooden ladder and popped my nose out into a scene from Hades' nightmare.

Our ship was leaning at a terrible angle as we climbed up a mountain of water. The wind was bellowing like a wounded bull. The thin mast of *The Pawgo* was shaking like a prisoner on execution day.

"Pawsidon must be angry," said Maxi. "This storm is getting worse."

Suddenly, the rocking stopped and we seemed to hang in mid air for a moment. Fighting the sick feeling in my stomach, I clung on with my claws. Down we fell, down from the crest of the great wave and into a bottomless pit of water. The cold sea rushed over my eyes and hit me with an unstoppable force. The claws on my right paw were ripped from their sockets and I held on with one paw, screaming. A felt a paw on my collar, dragging me back from a watery grave. A lightning flash lit the sky. Furia let go of my collar. I wish I could say that I thanked her for saving my life but I forget my manners when I am face to face with death.

"We're lost! We're lost!" I spluttered.

Lightning zigzagged across the sky, bursting the blackness. I looked down into the whirling waters, lit up by the flashes. I would not have been surprised if Hades himself was waiting there, ready to welcome us into the Underworld

But we were not dead yet. Somehow, *The Pawgo* struggled back out of the watery pit and ever so slowly, we began to crawl up the face of the next wave.

White fire flashed again and in front of me I could see another enormous wave, a great dark cliff of water.

The Pawgo began to inch its way up the face of this next monster.

"The ship can't take too much more of this!" cried Maxi, through the blasting wind.

"Hold on!" boomed Father Felinious.

"I can't" I moaned.

But somehow I held on.

This nightmare went on and on. Time after time we climbed the great cliffs of water. Again and again we hung helpless at the top of each wave, staring death in its watery face before plunging down.

I remember thinking of my father's advice to look for the good in everything. He was a fluff brain! Where was the good in this? "At least things can't get any worse," I sighed to myself.

"Rocks!" called Maxi in a panic. When the next flash of lightning lit up the sky, I saw two dark towers of rock looming up in front of me.

"Tiller!" cried the Father. "Steer to the left."

I remember Maxi at the back of the boat, heaving the tiller – the long pole that we used to steer *The Pawgo*.

"I can't hold it!" he cried.

Then I knew we were lost.

I closed my eyes and let go of the rail, hoping to find Summerlands. Then something strange happened. The force of the great wave saved us. Somehow *The Pawgo* was lifted up as the wave broke. It was thrown right over the jagged towers of rock and into the shelter of a quiet cove.

Hope Floats

"*The Pawgo* is wrecked," said Maxi. "There's no way we can fix this."

He was right. We'd survived last night's storm but our ship hadn't been so lucky. Her mast was broken and her sail flapped in the wind like a tattered rag.

"Shouldn't we all start looking for food?" I asked, eyeing up a dead jellyfish that had been washed up on the beach.

I was starving: I hadn't had a decent meal since we'd left Rome.

"Felinious didn't say anything about food," said Maxi, pawing at a dead crab. "But Furia has gone to look for water."

"I wish Felinious had sent us instead of her," I moaned.

"He didn't send her," said Maxi. "She went of her own accord."

Maxi sniffed at the stinky crab but decided not to chance it.

"Why are we doing this?" I muttered, throwing another plank of driftwood on the pile.

"Who knows!" said Maxi. "Felinious wants us to pile up all of the wood that we can find on the beach."

"I expect he wants us to get a fire going," I said. "I'm good with fires. Let's surprise him!"

Hope Burns

"Fool! Flea-brain! Ginger menace!" spat Felinious. I thought I saw tears in Felinious' green eyes as puffs of black smoke from the crackling fire blew into his face.

"We were only trying to help!" moaned Maxi. We thought you wanted the wood for a fire. We wanted to surprise you."

"Look around you!" roared Felinious, bristling with rage. "How many trees do you see on this island?"

"None," moaned Maxi. The island was rocky and barren. There wasn't a single tree as far as the eye could see.

"So where in the name of mighty Mewpiter did you think we were going to get wood to repair *The Pawgo*?" he continued. "You've burned our precious wood. All of it!"

It was too late to put the fire out. At first the wet wood had resisted, but now it was giving itself willingly to the flames.

"What shall we do now?" I asked.

Felinious gazed out over the flat blue sea.

"Do what you like," he hissed, then he stalked off down the beach.

The Beam

The Father had stalked off to lick his wounds. Furia had still not returned. My hope was shrivelling like a dead jellyfish on the beach. How could I have been so stupid?

To make things worse, what was left of *The Pawgo* had been washed off the rocks by the rising tide and now it lay nearby, on a bank of sand. Maxi thought it would float free on the next tide. But without wood to repair our ship we were stuck. We'd swapped a watery grave for a prison of sand.

My mouth was dry and cracked. Furia still hadn't returned. I wondered if she'd found any water on her search.

Maxi and I decided to go and find some more wood and make up for our mistake.

"Let's look further up the beach," said

Maxi. "If there was any wood washed up by last night's storm we are sure to find it there."

One thing I like about Maxi is his unstoppable confidence. I nodded and followed him up the beach.

"Shells, shells, shells!" I said. "But not a single piece of wood."

"Keep looking," said Maxi in a commanding voice. "We are sure to find some wood soon, I know it!"

But he was wrong. We walked for a mile up the beach before deciding to turn back.

"Cheer up Spartan!" said Maxi. "I'll race you back."

"I'm not racing!" I replied. But before the words had left my mouth, Maxi was running. He shot off like an arrow from a bow. I chased him, desperately trying to catch up. I was gaining ground. We were nearly back when Maxi tripped and fell head over paws.

"Miaaowch!" he moaned.

"I won! I won! Maxipuss is defeated!" I laughed, crossing an imaginary finish line.

Maxi wasn't pleased.

"You'll pay for that Spartan!" he

boomed. "I was winning! But I tripped over this..."

He stopped in the middle of his sentence. I padded up to him and saw what had stopped him in his tracks. It was an old wooden beam, as brown as the stones on the beach. It was half buried under the golden sand.

"Wood!" I cried. "Let's dig it out!"

With both of us digging it was easy to uncover. When one end of the beam was out, Maxi grabbed it with both paws and pulled hard.

"Lend a paw, Spartan!" said Maxi.

"Alright," I said, trying to get a grip.

"Come on! I'm pulling harder than you!" he added.

He was probably right but it is most annoying when your friends keep pointing out that they are better than you at stuff.

I pulled twice as hard and nearly lost a claw, tearing at the old wood.

"For the love of Affleana!" moaned Maxi. "This thing is never going to move."

Then something happened that is so strange that it sounds impossible when I write it down. As soon as these words left Maxi's mouth, I heard a strange voice calling over the sound of the waves. The voice sounded as old as the ragged rocks.

"Pull harder!" it said.

I dropped the wood, almost falling over in surprise.

Maxi heard it too, he sprang towards me with a look of amazement on his face.

"Dig me out!" demanded the strange voice. "I'm stuck!"

Maxi looked at the beam and turned towards me in amazement.

"You're... not going to believe this Spartan. But... I think there's someone trapped under that beam!"

Just then I heard a familiar voice:

"Students!" it called.

Looking up, I saw Father Felinious padding towards us. His voice crashing like one of Mewpiter's thunderbolts.

"Students! What are you doing?" he shouted.

"Coming Felinious!" I cried. But the voice called out to me again.

"Where do you think you're going?" it demanded. "Dig me out! I'm stuck down here!"

I looked at Maxi and he stared back at me, his eyes were wide with amazement. We grabbed hold of the plank again and gave it another massive pull. At last it came free. Maxi and I collapsed in a heap.

I blinked, wiping the sand from my coat. There before me was a thick beam of grey wood, about the same length as the wooden swords we use to practice.

The weather worn piece of wood was very old. When I got most of the sand and seaweed off, I saw that it was beautifully carved but the designs weren't Roman.

"Is that it?" sniffed Maxi, snatching the beam.

He wasn't impressed. I think he'd been hoping for a magical sword or a talking shield or a skeleton key. In fact, almost anything would have been more interesting than an old bit of wood. You could hear the disappointment in his voice. He held the piece of wood up at eye level.

"Talk!" he demanded. "Say something, like you did before."

But the old beam didn't answer. There was only the cry of the seagulls and the rush of the empty wind. Our talking beam was as silent as the grave.

"Gladiators!!!" boomed a voice like thunder.

It was only Father Felinious. "Maxipuss! Son of Spartapuss! Get over here right now!"

Disappointed, Maxi threw the beam down and padded off down the beach towards Felinious. I was about to follow him but something made me pick up the ancient beam before I left.

"What have you two flea-bags been up to?" asked Felinious. "Some new mischief I expect. You look as guilty as a couple of wolves in a sheep shed."

Before we could answer, he went on.

"Listen!" he said. "I have important news. Where is Furia? She needs to hear this too."

Maxi shrugged.

"She went to look for water. She's still not back," he said.

"We thought she was with you," I added. Felinious' tail began to flick in anger.

"Well you two may as well hear this anyway," he began. "We are not alone on this island. There is a port about half a day's walk along the beach. I've even met the locals."

"Thank Paws!" I cried. "We are saved!"

"Not quite," said Felinious. "They will not give us food or water. Not unless we can pay for it – which of course we can't."

"For Peus sake!" I moaned. "What kind of place is this?"

"This is the Island of Knossos," said the Father. As a rule, the Squeaks are famously kind and generous to strangers – but not on this island. The king here is famous for being the meanest cat in all of the Squeak Islands.

"What's his name?" I asked.

"King Minos," replied the Father.

"King *Meanos* is more like it," I moaned.

"Didn't you tell them we are Romans,

on our way to The Olympuss Games?" asked Maxi. "Everyone loves the games. That might have changed their minds?"

"That dog won't hunt," sighed Felinious. "I tried begging and explaining but they said they could not spare a single sardine or a sip of water. Their king is famous for his short paws and his long pockets."

Felinious turned and looked out to sea. The sun was melting into a burning teardrop as it dipped under the horizon. A band of purple and red filled the sky. It really was the most beautiful sunset I'd ever seen in my life. However, the only thing I could think about was my grumbling belly. I was so hungry that I wouldn't say no to a cold plate of dog food.

"Never give up hope," said Felinious. "Every mountain moves if you use the right lever."

"What in Paws' name is that supposed to mean?" hissed Maxi.

"It means that there is one thing that even mean King Minos will pay for," said Father Felinious. He patted Maxi on the back and smiled a sly smile. "There is one thing that they are starved of on this lonely island. We have it. And they will pay for it in gold."

Let The Games Begin!

"Entertainment?" I asked, blinking in the sharp morning sunlight.

"What did Felinious mean when he said they were 'starved of entertainment'?"

"We are the entertainment!" said Maxi. "If I know Father Felinious he'll have some kind of competition in mind. The Squeaks love the sports of boxing and wrestling. I expect he's planning on putting on a match."

After a freezing night on the hard beach, the only thing I wanted to wrestle with was a large breakfast. The cold had been bitter through the night, rising up through my paws and sinking deep into my bones. I had thought about burning the mysterious wooden beam but something stopped me. I decided that if it didn't speak again by nightfall, I'd definitely turn it into a campfire.

Just then, I spotted Father Felinious. He

was padding up the beach towards us, at the head of a proud group of cats. Behind Felinious came four cats in flowing robes carrying a golden chair. Sitting on the chair was a ginger and white cat who was as thin as a blade. He had angry eyes, not unlike a cobra that has just been poked with a sharp stick. On his head he wore a golden crown made from laurel leaves.

"Look!" said Maxi. "That must be mean King Minos."

His haggard face said it all. King Minos looked like the sort of cat who wouldn't save his own grandmother from a burning building unless she agreed to pay the water bill in advance.

The four servants who carried the royal chair were big and ugly.

"Wrestling eh?" I said to Maxi. "I don't fancy my chances against that lot."

"Don't fret Spartan," said Maxi. "The bigger they come the faster they'll run when the mighty Maxipuss steps into the arena."

My friend flexed his claws confidently. I was impressed with his spirit, but would it be enough to beat King Minos' minions?

As the royal party came closer, I listened carefully. Felinious was talking to the King. A long time ago my father gave me some advice about speaking truthfully to the powerful. "They might look like you and me, but kings are trouble. Keep your mouth shut," he told me. "If you want to have a tongue that can still lick."

Felinious grinned like an eel on a fish seller's slab. He was trying to sweet talk King Minos. It wasn't working but he carried on anyway.

"Have I seen your face before, Roman?" asked King Minos, sipping cream from a silver bowl (but not offering it around).

"I've got one of those familiar faces your greatness," said Felinious. "Pull ten Romans out of the Furum at random and you'll find five that look just like me."

The King glared at Felinious.

"Roman!" he hissed. "Where are these great fighters that you've been chattering about?"

"King Minos," said the Father. "Let me introduce you to the pride of Rome. The fighter they call Maxipuss the Magnificent."

Maxi raised his paw and waved an imaginary sword in the air. It was annoying but I had to admit that he looked like a winner.

"What about that one?" said the King, pointing a royal paw in my direction.

"Maxipuss will put on a great show," continued Felinious.

But the King was having none of it.

"That one over there!" he hissed. "The ginger."

"The ginger?" sighed Felinious. He obviously didn't think I could win "That's the one they call 'The Spartan'."

"That little rat?" laughed the King. "He hasn't got a drop of Spartan blood in him! He looks more like a dish licker than a killer."

I admit that I didn't look my best. The salty air was doing strange things to my fur. But I puffed up my tail and drew myself up to my fullest height. Then I put out my claws and fixed the King with a iron glare.

"Don't overdo it," hissed Felinious under his breath. "Maxi stands a better chance against this lot than you do."

"Let the contest begin!" ordered the

King impatiently.

"Wait!" said Felinious, holding a paw up before the King's slave hit the starting gong.

"First let us agree the rules. If Rome wins then the mighty King Minos will pay us a prize of one hundred silver coins..."

The King's green eyes flashed and he let out a low hiss.

"... which we will spend in the King's shops, buying food and repairing our ship."

The King nodded and smiled. He couldn't lose. Even if we won, he could charge as much as he wanted for the repairs.

"Pantheras!" called King Minos.

Up stepped a black cat with a long spear in his paw.

"Meet Pantheras," laughed the King, "He's my champion."

Every King needs a champion. In ancient times a king would fight every battle himself. The king would be the strongest warrior in his land. He defended his crown with his teeth and his claws. But that was no way to grow a country. The king would not rule for long. There would be many challengers, wanting to take the crown. So it became the custom that the King would select a champion, to fight for him.

Pantheras looked at me like a snake eyeing up a baby bird that has fallen out of its nest.

"Let us have a fair fight!" said Felinious.

"Pantheras hates Romans," laughed King Minos.

"Are we fighting to the death my lord?" asked Pantheras, padding forward with his claws out.

"Take this Roman rat apart," laughed Minos. "Make him die, but take your time. I want value for money."

I looked at Felinious, fighting the urge to run.

"So be it!" said Felinious. "Your wish is my command."

King Minos rubbed his shabby paws together and let out a little mew of excitement. Did he enjoy watching strangers die? Or perhaps he was imagining how good my ginger fur would look as a rug on his bedroom floor. I expect that floor was cold, judging by the lack of firewood on the island.

I turned to Felinious in horror. But

before I could protest, he spoke again.

"Of course, a death match will cost you more money. Two hundred denari, win or lose. But it is a small price to pay for such fine sport."

"Two hundred Roman coins?" hissed King Minos. His thin tail beat the ground. I thought he was going to kill Felinious on the spot. But Felinious kept his cool.

"For a death match you must pay, even if we lose," explained Felinious.

The King looked like a fish farmer who has just spotted a hole in one of his nets.

"Trained gladiators cost money," explained Felinious.

We waited for the King's decision. My fate was hanging in the balance. The sun blazed yellow. The sky was the same blue as before. But everything had changed, now my life was on the line.

"Get on with it!" hissed King Minos. "Do I have to wait all day?"

But what had he decided? Was it going to be a fight to the death or not?

The beach fell silent. My tail flicked over the hot sand. I saw the thoughts in Felinious' head. He had already pushed

King Minos a long way. The wrong word to the King could get all of us killed. Felinious opened his mouth but the river of words had dried up.

One of the King's guards stepped forward. He was an ancient looking tabby with thick grey whiskers like dried reeds. He was carrying a beaten up gong. He banged it with a feeble blow. The gong didn't ring out proudly, it made the sort of clank that a metal dinner bowl makes when you drop it on a stone floor.

The King's guards had marked out a circle with white stones. The pebbles showed the edge of the ring. If you were thrown and landed outside the circle, you would lose. The guards stood ready to prevent escape.

My opponent padded towards me.

"Hey Spartan!" called a voice.

"What do you want Maxi?" I asked.

"If you die, I will avenge you!" said Maxi. "I swear it."

"Thanks," I said. "But I was hoping for some advice. Anything that could help me beat Pantheras."

Maxi thought for a moment but then he just smiled and shrugged.

Pantheras circled me, dancing the age old dance of the trained fighter. He was a big cat but he seemed to pour himself from move to move. There was a natural grace in his movements – the effortless flow that comes from years of practice.

Pantheras sprang towards me, his eyes flashing, striking at my face with his left paw. I dodged his claws, remembering to look out for an attack from the right. Seeing that I was ready to block his next blow, Pantheras rocked back and waited, crouching like a hungry snake at a rat's front door. At last he darted forward. The blow connected with my shoulder and slammed me towards the very edge of the circle. I almost touched the white stones, but rolled back inside the circle just in time.

"Step out of the ring and you will be defeated," warned Felinious.

I didn't need reminding.

Pantheras let out a low growl and came at me again. He unsheathed his claws. I've seen shorter kitchen knives.

A tide of fear turned within me. Dark thoughts gathered in my mind. What was I doing here? Where was Furia? She should be fighting Pantheras, not me.

Another strike ripped against my face and it sent me spinning. In a panic I rolled away. Then I heard the clang of the clapped out gong and I looked down. One of my back paws was outside the circle.

"We win! We win!" cried King Minos.

Patheras gazed adoringly at his King.

King Minos threw him his own sword. Its polished silver blade caught the light.

"Finish the Roman!" he commanded.

As Pantheras advanced towards me, I caught the look on his face. He had sad eyes, for a professional killer.

"Wait!!!" called a voice. It was Felinious.

"What for?" cried King Minos, bristling.

"It's two hundred denari if your champion kills the Spartan. Two hundred coins, win or lose. That is what we agreed my lord," reminded Felinious.

Pantheras raised his sword. I waited, my heart still pumping after the fight. My blood had turned to fire. Every nerve burned inside me.

Dragging my eyes from Pantheras' gaze, I searched the beach for something that could save me. Stooping to the floor, I shot out my paw and picked up the beam of carved ash that Maxi and I had found the evening before. The wood felt warm to the touch. I could hardly believe it when I heard myself saying.

"Wooden beam, help me now! I saved you from the sands. Now it's your turn to help me."

But the old oak beam did not answer.

As Pantheras raised his knife, ready to finish me, Felinious turned to King Minos.

"Two hundred denari for his life," said Felinious again. "Roman gladiators don't come cheap."

Pantheras looked at his King, waiting for the word.

"Leave him!" commanded King Minos.

I dropped to the floor, still holding the wooden beam in my paw.

"Thank you my lord," said Felinious.

"Don't thank me," said King Minos. "Everything of yours is mine. Even that wreck you call a ship."

"But our ship is of no value," said Felinious.

"Everything you own!" said King Minos.

He leaped from the chair and padded towards me. I thought he was going to kill me himself. But he snatched the beam from my grasp.

"Every last thing!" he said. "Even this."

Mean King Minos

"It's a good thing Minos is the meanest King in the Mediterranean," said Maxi.

"Why is that?" I sighed.

"Because if that old goat wasn't such a

tight paw, you'd be as dead as dog meat by now!" he laughed.

Maxi was right. Felinious had saved me. When he'd been reminded that he'd have to pay extra for a death match, King Minos had spared my life. If it wasn't for Felinious, Queen Minos would be wearing ginger gloves this winter.

At that moment, the door of the cage opened and a familiar figure stalked in.

"Furia!" I said in amazement. "What are you doing here?"

"Eating treats with Queen Candmeet!" she said sarcastically. "What do you think I'm doing?"

"They captured you too?" sighed Maxi. "That's a pity. I was just saying that while you were free, there was still hope."

Furia's tail began to flick but she said nothing. It was Felinious who spoke next.

"Where were you when we needed you?" he sighed. "You could have defeated Pantheras."

Furia didn't answer. She sat motionless, but I knew that under the still pools of her eyes, her thoughts were raging.

"So it's a life of honest work for us," I

said. "I suppose it could be worse."

Father Felinious let out a little mew. He looked like a broken cat.

"What are you moaning about?" said an old guard with a nose like a rotten apple. He poked something though the bars. The Father picked it up. It was a wooden flute.

"Can you play the flute?" asked the guard.

"Me? No!" said Felinious.

"Then you'll have to work like the rest of the strays," laughed the guard.

"Work?" gasped the Father. "Me?"

Furia sprang at him and pressed her face towards his face until their whiskers were almost touching.

"Stars of Asteria!" she hissed. "I cannot believe you Romans!' You capture us. You say you own us. You make us fight. But when the boot is on the other paw, you cry like spoilt kittens."

"You are young Furia," said Felinious. "I am too old to be a slave!"

"Hush!" said a voice from the other side of the wooden bars. I looked up to see a familiar face. It was an ancient looking cat that I'd noticed earlier. He had a spear in his paw but there was no hate in his eyes.

"Who are you?" demanded Maxi. "And why are you keeping us caged up like rabbits?"

"My name is Androclaws," replied the ancient cat. "A word of advice from a cat who has seen many summers. It would be better for you if you accept your situation."

"What do you mean?" asked Maxi.

"Don't think of yourselves as slaves," advised Androclaws, "think of yourselves as builders."

"Builders?" said Maxi in surprise. "That does have a better ring to it. But what are we building?"

Androclaws took a worn bronze key from the loop on his belt and unlocked the cage door.

"Follow me and you'll find out. It's a sight that few Romans have ever seen," he said.

Furia's tail flicked angrily against the dusty floor. She always hates it when she is mistaken for a Roman.

"Come!" said Androclaws. "You are about to see a wonderful sight. It's better than The Colossal Colossus of Knossos!!"

"The Colossal... what?" I asked.

Androclaws gasped.

"Surely you've heard of The Colossal Colossus of Knossos? It's one of the seven wonders of the world."

"Sorry!" I said. "I've never heard of it."

Androclaws looked stunned.

"It's a statue of a cat," said Maxi. "A really big statue. It's wearing a golden hat."

"Great!" I said, trying to sound enthusiastic.

The Slobberynth

Before we could work, we had to walk. With Androclaws leading the way, we set off with the weak morning sun on our backs. As the sun climbed its invisible ladder into the sky, the heat began to build. As the miles passed I saw nothing but rocks and stones and the guts of a ruined temple lost in weeds. We passed a cluster of olive trees. Their trunks were bent like fish hooks and they looked too shrivelled to produce fruit. There was still no sign of water anywhere.

We padded on and on. The heat began

to build until it was hotter than Hades' bath. The hot wind blasted my nose. The sand below my paws was burning. Slowly, I struggled on. We Kitons are not built for this sort of heat. Androclaws did not seem to mind. He even hummed a little tune as he padded through the red dust.

"How far is it now?" I gasped, but the words came out in a slur. My tongue had stuck to the roof of my mouth. It was drier than a dead camel's hump.

Far away in the distance a faint line appeared on the horizon. It was a slightly redder shade than the rest of the landscape. As we inched towards it, it grew bigger and bigger until it filled my sight. We had reached a great wall made of red stone. It was completely smooth except for a long design that snaked along the wall at triple head height like a battle scar.

"Behold!" said Androclaws.

"Behold what?" gasped Maxi, wiping the dust from his eyes with his paws.

Androclaws' eyes burned fiercely. This gentle old cat got angry faster than anyone I've met.

"Behold the Slobberynth!" he bellowed,

sweeping his paw in a smooth arc to show off how long the wall was. But it was a sight that didn't need sweeping gestures.

Androclaws got out a bronze whistle and blew three times. The gates swung open. A curtain of dust slowly settled. When I close my eyes now, the sight hangs in the halls of my memory. All I could taste was the red dust. All I could smell was the black smoke from the fires and furnaces. Everything shook to the noise of a hundred hammers. It was as if Vulcan the blacksmith was holding an iron bashing competition. Gangs of workers ran around like angry ants – but ants seem to know where they are going. These workers were rushing about the place, hissing at the tops of their voices. Calling for water, calling for bricks and stones, calling for tools. And all of them were working for mean King Minos, to rebuild the walls of his mighty Slobberynth.

The Slobberynth is the biggest maze that I've ever seen. Actually, it's the only maze I've ever seen, but it was vast. It was old too, as old as the hills of Knossos.

Some of you probably don't care for

old things. I expect that you would rather have a shiny new collar than an old one. Me too! But King Minos loved old things with a passion that most cats save for their kittens. It was the King's life's work to restore the ancient maze – the Slobberynth – to its former glory. Well, I say 'his life's work' but in fact he had hundreds of slaves doing it for him. Minos used his workers like a carpenter uses tools. But when King Minos had finished with his tools, he didn't need to put them back in the box. They got up and walked back to their work camp of their own accord.

Old Androclaws must have been a mind reader. Later as we sat drinking water from our wooden bowls he turned to me and spoke.

"Thinking about escaping?" he asked.

"Of course not!" I answered in a wounded voice.

"Good my friend," he replied, "because I must warn you that The Slobberynth is guarded."

Looking around me, I noticed two tall stone towers where guards were on duty. They were wilting in the heat, leaning on their long spears. I felt sorry for them, having to stand guard in this dust bowl.

"I'm not talking about the guards!" said Androclaws in a low voice. "Believe me my friend, you do not want to meet the guardian that watches the maze for King Minos."

"What do you mean?" I asked.

"Hang on," said Maxi. "Are you saying that there is some sort of creature that walks The Slobberynth at night?"

"I am not saying anything Roman," said Androclaws. "But keep your ears open tonight and you will hear it."

"Bored yet?" I asked.

Maxi let out a purr of pleasure as he swung his hammer and smashed another block of stone.

"ARE YOU BORED YET?" I shouted at the top of my voice.

"What?" cried Maxi, swinging the iron hammer again.

It was midday. The Slobberynth was hotter than Hades with the heating on. But Maxi had a smile on his face. Not because he enjoyed the work but because he was better than me at smashing blocks.

I picked up my hammer. Maxi had taken the biggest one. My paw trembled as I lifted it up. I let out a grunt as I swung the hammer down into the block of stone with all my strength.

The hammer bounced when it hit the stone and it leapt out of my paw.

When the dust had cleared, I saw that the stone block had not broken in two. In fact there was hardly a mark on it.

"Hit it harder Spartan!" laughed Maxi, trashing another rock.

"Want to swap rocks?" I asked. "I'm bored with this one."

"Sorry," said Maxi. "I'm on a roll."

Smashing up rocks might have been Maxi's dream job, but it wasn't mine!

A gong signalled that it was time for our water break. I lapped up the muddy water but it didn't quench my thirst. In the beat of a butterfly's wing we were working again.

Our task was to repair a massive hole in the wall of the maze. A cat called Daedapuss was in charge of our work gang. He had a whip on his belt but I never saw him use it. I got the feeling that he wasn't really that strict, but he had to report to Pantheras. The very same Pantheras who had defeated me in yesterday's gladiator battle. Being the King's champion was only Pantheras' part time job. Mean King Minos also used him to whip the workers into shape.

Daedapuss had a sagging face and his nose was as flat as a strap. Perhaps someone had dropped a rock on it? Daedapuss was pleased with Maxi's stone bashing, but he wasn't happy with my work. He accused me of time wasting. But

I was breaking rocks as fast as I could!

The day closed like a clam. As darkness fell I could smell fish and shellfish grilling on a barbecue. My spirits lifted at the delicious smells.

"Dream on Roman!" scoffed Daedapuss. "That meal is for King Minos. His champion Pantheras might get to lick the bowl out. But the likes of us have to live on this."

He filled a bowl with greasy grey soup. It was all water apart from a lone bean, stranded in the middle like a drowning sailor.

"Is that all there is to eat?" moaned Maxi when I passed him his dinner.

"That's your lot," hissed Daedapuss.

"I've seen larger portions on a bird table!" snapped Maxi. "How are we going to live on this?"

"You will have to make do," said Daedapuss. "Unless..."

His voice suddenly died to a whisper.

"Unless what?" demanded Maxi angrily.

"Unless, you want to spend your wages on more food at the shop."

"The shop?" I said in surprise. "What

kind of King has a shop?"

"King Minos is very proud of his shop," said Daedapuss. "He says every great temple must have one. But..."

He shrugged his shoulders and stopped in mid sentence.

"But what?" asked Maxi.

Daedapuss screwed up his leathery nose and spoke in a low whisper.

"They don't call him 'mean King Minos' for nothing," he hissed. "The prices he charges are a disgrace."

Black Night

That night I was more tired than I can remember. The long walk in the sun and half a day of stone smashing had drained the life out of me. I was ready to sleep for a week.

"Where do we sleep?" I asked.

"Anywhere," said Daedapuss.

"Aren't you going to lock us up for the night?" I asked.

I was used to the locked doors at the gladiator school.

"No need," said Daedapuss. "But if

you are thinking about escaping, put that thought out of your mind. Death walks this maze at night."

Those words did not stop me from falling into a deep sleep. Later that night I was woken by a vibration that set my whiskers on edge. Slowly, I opened my eyes. The yellow moon hung in the sky, glowing like a temple lamp. Sitting totally still, I caught a sudden movement along the passageway. I sprang silently forwards and padded after the shadow as quickly as I dared. Turning the corner, I saw a shape. Familiar white face markings stood out in the moonlight.

"Furia!" I gasped. "What are you doing?"

"Baking buns for Queen Boudicat!" she snapped. "What do you think I'm doing?"

Ever since we'd first set a paw on *The Pawgo*, Furia had been looking to escape. We had seen very little of her since our arrival. She and Felinious had joined a different work group. I hadn't had time to pass on the warnings of Androclaws and Daedapuss. They'd said it was 'death' to go into the maze at night. But that sort of a warning would never stop Furia.

Her orange eyes flashed at me and her tail thumped against the cold stone floor.

Then she said something unexpected. Something that made me gasp.

"Coming?" she asked.

I stood there, tongue tied as Furia's fiery eyes flashed at me. I was amazed and honoured. Furia wanted me to escape with her.

"Yes!" I said gratefully. Then my heart sank. "But Androclaws and Daedapuss both said that it is dangerous. And what should we do about Maxi and Father Felinious?"

Furia shrugged off these questions.

"Come on if you're coming!" she hissed.

Furia padded off into the night and I followed her. Wind as warm as blood rushed down the passage towards the unknown heart of the Slobberynth. There was no roof, so the old maze was open to the sky. By some trick of the light the silver of the moonlight seemed to turn a ghostly green as it bounded off the ancient walls.

We padded on, passing passageways to the left and to the right. I was honoured that Furia wanted me to come with her. But I was feeling guilty about leaving Maxi. It didn't seem right to dump him here, even though he seemed to like smashing up rocks.

On we padded. I'd counted six crossroads now. I hoped that Furia knew what she was doing.

I was relieved when she stopped. I caught my breath, trying not to make a noise. This must be what writers mean when the say that the silence was 'heavy'.

"Furia?" I whispered. "How can you tell we are going the right way?"

She pointed at a spot on the wall. At first glance it looked exactly like the rest of the wall. Then I saw an outline taking shape against the mossy green of the crumbling wall. I ran my paw against the stonework, tracing the carved outline of a single lidless eye.

"It's the Cyclaw," I said, pointing to the picture of the famous one eyed giant. "That's easy to remember."

Furia nodded.

"This way!" she commanded. "Move in silence, you stomp like a baby elephant."

As I followed Furia, I struggled to

remember the route we'd taken. I racked my brain. We'd taken the left passage at the Cyclaw carving, and that was the sixth crossroads that we'd passed. I usually trust my instincts about directions but every part of this maze looked the same.

As these thoughts chased around my brain like frightened rabbits, my paw came down on something hard. Alarmed, I stepped back. There in the moonlight was a white skull. I looked on in horror, my eyes locked onto the empty sockets where the dead creature's eyes had once blinked.

"Paws protect us!" I gasped.

My frightened shout bounced off the walls and echoed down the empty passage.

Furia glared at me, her eyes burning.

"Silence!" she hissed.

I backed away from the pile of white bones, trying not to bristle in fear. It was no use, my fur was already standing up. My tail was as wide as a carpet brush.

"Sorry Furia," I whispered, backing away from the pale skeleton. "I don't like skulls..."

It was not a wise thing to say, I admit. I have never met a cat who likes skeletons. Bones are for dogs.

Furia ignored me and sprang off into the maze again. A terrible noise tore through the silence and came echoing towards us.

Furia and I stood like statues, lit by the light of the bright moon.

"What in Paws's name was that?" I whispered.

Furia shrugged. Her body had stiffened, ready for an attack.

"Where is that noise coming from..." I began. But I was interrupted as the horrible roaring struck up again.

"I'm sorry Furia!" I gasped. "I think I've

disturbed something. What are we going to do now?"

Furia looked left and right, her whiskers quivering in the still night air.

"Run!" she hissed.

Furia shot off like an arrow from a bow. I followed like cold porridge from a spoon. I was too frightened to run. Soon I was struggling to keep up. I wanted to cry out: "Wait! Wait for me!" but fear had got my tongue.

Whatever was out there would surely hear me if I cried out. So I kept silent as a river of fear rose within me. Furia was out of sight now but I could hear her somewhere up ahead.

In a panic I tried to remember the way back. How many passages had I passed? Was it five? Or six? I'd lost count.

"Furia..." I began. But my instincts strangled the shout before it left my mouth. It would be madness to make any more noise now.

I stopped running and caught my breath. This part of the maze was completely dark. The moon was wrapped in cloud. It was as silent as the grave. The only sound was the thumping of my heart. Then I saw a movement in the shadows ahead.

Shaking with dread, I crouched by the stone wall. Whatever was out there was about to come around the corner. I was trapped like a rat in a rock snake's den. The shadow spread slowly towards me.

"Spartan?" called a voice.

"Maxi!" I gasped. "Thank Paws!"

As he came nearer, I saw that there was another cat at his side.

"Quickly Spartan!" said Maxi. "Androclaws says that the Slobberynth is not safe tonight."

Androclaws groomed his long whiskers and nodded.

"Thanks," I gasped, surprised that the grumpy old Squeak had bothered to leave his bed for my sake.

"The older you get, the harder it is to sleep through the night," sighed Androclaws. "Do you know where you are?"

"Sort of.." I replied.

Maxi let out a long loud laugh. It was too loud and too long for my liking.

"You don't have a clue where you are, do you Spartan?" he said.

Annoyingly, he was right. I was completely lost.

"Follow me! Quickly!" ordered Androclaws. "It is not safe to walk the Slobberynth at night."

I wanted him to explain but I decided that now wasn't the right time.

"Which way?" I asked, trying to keep the fear out of my voice.

At that moment I noticed that Androclaws was holding a ball of string. Maxi starred longingly at it.

"Follow me!" ordered Androclaws.

Holding up the ball of string, he began to retrace his steps, winding the string back onto the ball as he went.

"That's clever," I said. "You're using the string to lead us back to where we started."

Androclaws nodded.

We walked for what seemed like an age before I spotted a familiar sight.

"The Cyclaw!" I said, pointing at the carving. "This is the way back."

"You were nearly lost for good," warned Androclaws. "The Slobberynth was designed to suck you in like a whirlpool. It makes you second guess yourself. It was designed that way."

I was about to ask him why it wanted to suck you in, when I heard that dreadful noise again, roaring through the night like distant thunder.

"Come," said Androclaws, we are nearly home."

"Thank you Androclaws. You've saved my life tonight. How can I repay you?"

The old ginger tom laughed.

"If I've stopped you from throwing your young life away – then that is all the reward I need," he said.

I half expected him to ask me if I had learned my lesson. But I am a slow learner, as you will soon find out.

The Stolen Collar

You may be wondering whether or not my fiery eyed friend Furia escaped from the maze. Don't worry! When we finally made it back to our camp, Furia was already there waiting for us. She was sitting on a rock, playing with the charms on her collar.

When she saw me, I noticed a flicker of an expression pass across her face. I'm not sure whether it was relief or annoyance.

I was too tired to tell Furia why you should not run off and leave your friends. So I dozed through what little was left of the night. It was a dreamless sleep. Maxi woke me a few hours later with a bowl of thin soup.

"Make it last Spartan," he said. "Daedapuss says that's all we are getting until dinner."

I put down the bowl of soup and looked him in the eye.

"So that's it then," I said.

"What do you mean?" he asked.

"That's it," I said again. "We can't escape from the Slobberynth. We are doomed to stay here for the rest of our days."

Maxi sighed and scratched at a spot under his chin.

"Never give up!" said a familiar voice.

It was Father Felinious. His tail was flicking but his eyes were kind. I thought he would be furious with me for trying to escape.

"Didn't you hear me Spartan?" he laughed, scratching his chin. "Never give up and never give in!"

Then he let out a little purr of satisfaction. I had no idea why he was so pleased with himself.

Rock On

The hours crawled past. I broke some more rocks. The sun blazed down on the Slobberynth, hotter than lava.

I will spare you the details about the rock breaking and the terrible heat but there was an awful lot of both. The pads on my paws were red and raw by the time the sun dipped below the horizon and it was finally time to go back to our camp for dinner.

I was hungry for soup that night. In fact I was hungry for anything. So imagine my surprise when I got back and found Father Felinious roasting a fish over a roaring fire.

"Share my feast friends!" he said, passing me a fish from a plate. "Eat! There is food for all."

I didn't stop to ask questions. I was too hungry. Maxi and I tore into our food like puppies in a bone pile.

"This is more like it!" laughed Maxi, with a fish in each paw. "Pass the sauce!"

Maxi reached for the saucepan and poured a helping over his fish.

"Where did you get all of this food Father Felinious?" I asked in amazement.

"At the store of course," replied Felinious.

"But where did you get the money?" I asked.

Felinious gave me a strange look.

"Let's just say that Fortune has smiled on us Spartan!" he said quietly.

He sat there, clutching a fish in one paw and holding a bowl of cream in the other. Then he passed the cream around and told us to drink.

It all seemed too good to be true. And as my father used to say, if things seem too good to be true, they usually are.

Liar's Feast

As quick as a bolt from Mewpiter, this happy scene was shattered. Furia stalked in, bristling with rage.

"Furia," said Maxi, with a mouth full of

fish. He was so busy eating that he hadn't noticed the desperate look on her face.

"Where is it?" she spat, bounding over and knocking the fish bowl out of his paw.

"Hey!" said Maxi. "What's your problem? I was enjoying that."

Suddenly, all the fire had left Furia's eyes. Her voice was as cold as winter.

"Where is it?" she demanded again. "Which one of you has taken it?"

Her tail slapped angrily against the sand.

"Where is what?" asked Maxi.

He was so hungry that he picked the fish up from the ground and carried on eating it.

"You know what I'm talking about," hissed Furia accusingly. "I hid my collar under a rock for safe keeping. When I looked in the hiding place this morning, my collar was gone."

We looked at her in silent amazement.

"One of you knows something," she muttered. "That collar means more to me than anything."

I noticed that Felinious had been sitting quietly during all of this.

"We're sorry my dear," said Felinious. "But have no fear, perhaps it will turn up."

I thought that she was going to kill him there and then, but instead she turned on me.

"It had better turn up," she hissed. "Or I'll turn you inside out!"

Without another word she stalked off into the night.

When she had gone we sat in silence. The fire was still hot, the food was still good but I had lost my appetite.

Maxi looked at Felinious.

"Are you sure you don't know anything about Furia's collar?" he asked.

Felinious did not answer, he just carried on sipping cream from his bowl as if nothing had happened.

Later that night, after Felinious had gone to his bed, I woke and saw Maxi. He was standing in a column of cold blue moonlight. A cloud of anger hung around him.

"Felinious is the collar thief," he whispered.

"What do you mean?" I gasped.

"It must have been him!" he said under

his breath. "How do you think he got the money to buy all of that food? I bet he stole it and sold it to King Minos."

I let out a little mew of surprise.

"I know that Felinious has a crafty side," I said. "But surely he wouldn't steal another cat's collar?"

"Wise up Spartan!" said Maxi. "Not everyone plays by your rules. Maybe they didn't teach 'Do as you would be done by' on the mean streets where Felinious grew up."

I hated to admit it, but Maxi was right again.

"So what are we going to do about it?" I asked.

Maxi's tail thumped impatiently against the cold ground.

In the distance, I could hear the gong calling King Minos' sleepy workers from their beds. Another day of work was about to begin.

"We've got to help Furia to get her collar back," said Maxi.

"It's too risky," I replied. "If Felinious sold the collar to King Minos, it'll be in the palace by now. Pantheras and the royal guards keep watch day and night."

"I know Spartan," said Maxi. "But there might be a way to sneak in and get it."

"What way?" I hissed. "There's no way Maxi. It's madness!"

"That sly old fox Felinious was right about one thing," said Maxi. "Never give up! Never give in!"

I had never heard Maxi sound this serious about anything.

The Daily Grind

A long day of smash and grind passed. I wondered who was using all of these rocks that we were bashing. In fact we were the first stage in a grand design. Far away on the north side of the camp, teams of master stone masons were using our blocks to fix the walls. The Slobberynth was rising again.

Maxi didn't say anything else about the stolen collar, but I knew that he was planning something. When the gong sounded for our final water break, I saw Maxi whisper something to Androclaws. I have good ears but even I could not make out what was said.

I wished I could snuff the day out like a candle. It seemed like an age before the rusty sun set and a silver moon was cast.

We drank our soup in silence and settled down for another cold night. I was woken by a voice whispering in my ear.

"Come on Spartan," said Maxi. "We're leaving."

We padded down the path as quietly as a couple of ghosts. A part of me felt relieved to be on the move but I could not stop thinking about the noises I'd heard the night before. If trying to escape again wasn't madness, it was not far off.

When we were finally out of ear shot of the camp, I spoke urgently.

"Maxi-," I began.

My heart was racing like a loose chariot horse.

"Relax Spartan!" laughed Maxi.

"I got completely lost in the maze last night," I said. "You heard the noises, didn't you?"

"It'll be different this time," he said.

"Why?" I asked flatly.

"You've got Maxipuss the Mighty as your guide," he said confidently.

I was not sure if he was serious.

"Great!" I sighed.

"And Androclaws gave me this."

He produced a brown woollen bag from under his coat.

"What's in the bag?" I asked.

"Freak handles," explained Maxi.

"What!" I hissed. "What in the name of mighty Peus are freak handles?"

Maxi scratched his chin and gave me a puzzled look.

"It beats me!" he said finally. "But Androclaws said we'd need them. He gave me this bag and told me never to go into the maze without freak handles.

I craned my neck up at the hole in the wall which marked the entry point into the Slobberynth. In a few seconds, we would be inside its walls again. I sniffed the air suspiciously.

"Follow me," said Maxi.

Maxi climbed up a pile of broken stones and through a gaping hole into the maze.

On the other side, the wall was crumbling. The ancient stones soaked up the moonlight like a sponge. They'd turned a grimy blue colour. Maxi moved off. I followed him for a few steps down the passage and then I hissed.

"Wait!" I said. "Aren't you going to open the bag?"

Maxi got the woollen bag out again and emptied it out onto the ground.

"Three candles!" I laughed. "Not freak handles."

Maxi wasn't smiling.

"What's the matter?" I asked.

"We don't have a light..."

At that moment I spotted a ghostly green glow at the far end of the passage. At first I thought my eyes were playing tricks on me. Then it was gone.

"Wait here!" he said. "Whatever you do, don't wander off!"

Maxi padded quietly down the passage, leaving me alone in the long darkness. The air tasted stale.

I strained my ears for noises but the maze was as quiet as a Fleagyptian tomb.

I heard Maxi's footsteps coming back. Then I saw the green glow again. Suddenly, Maxi rounded the corner. Alongside him was Furia, holding a flickering candle.

"Furia..." I began. "Listen, I'm sorry..."

"There's no time for that," she said. "Pass me a candle."

I did as I was told and Furia lit the first of the three candles. Carefully, she placed it in a spot away from the wall where the night wind could not blow it out.

"Clever," said Maxi. "We will light the candles and place them at points along our way. That means we'll be able to find our way back."

"I'm not coming back," hissed Furia. "Unless I come back to drive a spear into that rat Felinious."

Even though I didn't trust Felinious, I still felt bad about leaving him behind. But the look in Furia's eyes had answered my question before I asked it. So I kept my mouth shut.

"Let's go!" ordered Furia, padding silently down the passage.

The air felt damp tonight. I could feel a chill running through my claws. I stopped for a moment. Something held me rooted to the spot as the dancing candle moved further away from me. Its yellow flame had dimmed into a faint glow.

"Follow the candlelight," I said to

myself. "It will lead you home."

It flickered like a will-o'-the-wisp in the distance.

I have to admit that I had my doubts about Maxi's plan. The idea was that we would make our way through the maze and come out at the other side of the Slobberynth next to mean King Minos' palace. Then we would sneak past the guards, break in and steal Furia's collar. Then the three of us would go on the run. Where we were supposed to run to hadn't been decided yet. But I didn't speak up, mainly because I didn't have any better ideas.

"Wait!" I said in a voice lower than a whisper.

The others stopped in front of me.

Far away in the distance, I had heard a noise. Was it the sound of our own footsteps? The walls of the maze were crumbling, it could just have been a rock fall.

This part of the Slobberynth was dark. The moon had disappeared behind a cloud. The air smelled damp and unclean. Then the thudding noise started up again, and this time it got louder and louder, until the walls began to shake.

I coughed and choked. In the dim glow of the candle I saw clouds of dust coming off the shaking walls. A sound howled through the night. It was loud but distant, like thunder in the high mountains. The ground beneath my paws began to shake.

"Spartan!" called Maxi. "Come on!"

Maxipuss the Magnificent

Maxi and Furia were already running but the thunderous noise had glued me to the spot.

At last I sprang forwards, following Furia down a dark spider's web of passages, fleeing from that terrible noise.

My heart was beating like a blacksmith's hammer. The other two were faster than me. I heard the noise howl out again, closer this time.

I saw the bobbing lights getting fainter and fainter ahead of me. Maxi and Furia were racing ahead, disappearing into the gloom.

"Wait!" I called. "Wait for me!"

Then the light disappeared and I heard Maxi shout.

"Paws protect us!"

As I came rushing around the corner, I finally saw what had stopped Maxi and Furia in their tracks.

In front of me stood a giant figure. Its skin was a sickly green colour. Its eyes burned with a hot orange glow. It had the monstrous head of a bull, crowned with a pair of sharp golden horns.

Every kitten has heard stories of this legendary beast. Stories that sent them scuttling back to their baskets in terror. As a river of panic burst its banks, I mouthed the name of the monster.

"The Minopaw!" I gasped.

My heart was drumming. Fear swept over me. Seeing me bristle, Maxi drew closer.

"I know what you are thinking," he said, putting a friendly paw on my shoulder. "You want the honour of being the first to do battle with the Minopaw, don't you?"

I nodded. Actually I was thinking about running away as fast as my cowardly paws would carry me.

"Stay where you are Spartan!" Maxi said. "Keep well back, for this enemy is beyond your skill."

Furia rolled her eyes. Maxi had the heart of a tiger. He might also have the brain of a bullfrog, but he was right – I couldn't beat the Minopaw in a month of Mondays.

Maxi took his paw off my shoulder, extended his claws and bravely padded towards the enemy.

"Fear not! No foe, no matter how high

and mighty, is a match for the sword of Maxipuss!" he roared.

"But Maxi!" I gasped. "You don't have a sword."

"That doesn't matter!" he laughed. "I have these!"

Then he extended his claws, let out a wild yowl and charged at the Minopaw.

But the mighty Minopaw did not move. Its fiery eyes flickered, but it stood as still as a stone. I waited in horror, preparing for it to lift its muscle-bound arms and swat my brave friend like a gnat.

"For glory! And for Rome!" screamed Maxi, springing towards the beast.

When the clouds lifted from the moon, the room was filled with a cold light. I realised why the Minopaw wasn't moving. I'd been tricked! It was a statue – an enormous stone statue with flaming torches behind its eyes.

"Had enough Minopaw?" laughed Maxi. "Don't just stand there you blockhead. Fight me!"

I let out an angry yowl.

"Very funny!" I hissed. "I expect you are really pleased with yourself?"

Maxi collapsed on the ground, rolling in the dust and laughing as if it was the funniest thing he had ever seen in his life.

"I got you Spartan!" he roared. "I really got you!"

I let out a loud hiss and stepped towards him.

"Silence!" cried Furia. "You two are making enough noise to wake Hades. Let's take a closer look."

The great statue was just as impressive close up. In fact, it seemed to get bigger and bigger the closer you got to it. I went to touch the stonework but I pulled my paw back in a hurry. The old statue was covered in a grimy patchwork of cobwebs. Torchlight from behind the Minopaw's eyes bounced off the stone, lighting the room with a creepy orange glow.

"I wonder how they light those torches up there in its eyes?" I asked. "I suppose the statue must be hollow."

"Fight me Minopaw! Fight me!" said Maxi again, waving an imaginary sword through the air and laughing in my face.

"In Paw's name, will you stop that?" I spat." It isn't funny."

"Fleas of Affleana!" said Maxi, "Somebody can't take a joke!"

From deep inside the statue a voice as old as the hills boomed out:

"Trust to the wooden walls!"

We all stood as still as miniature stone Minopaws. Maxi was the first to speak.

"Who's there?" he demanded.

"The Oracle of Knossos," said the voice. "You have come to ask a question to the Oracle, haven't you?"

"To ask what?" I gasped, listening hard. The voice seemed to be coming from the belly of the statue.

"To ask the *Oracle*," replied the voice, getting impatient. "You want help or advice, and the Oracle gives it in the form of a clue. But I'm not supposed to just *tell* you the answer. I have to keep it cryptic."

"Cryptic?" asked Maxi.

"It means hidden," said Furia. "The Oracle can't give us an easy answer. It has to answer in the form of a riddle."

Maxi padded to a spot at the back of the monstrous statue and pointed upwards.

"Keep it talking," he whispered.

"What shall I say?" I asked.

"Anything you like," he snapped.

"What is your advice great Oracle of Knossos?" I asked.

"Trust to the wooden walls," repeated the voice. It was starting to sound rather annoyed.

"The wooden what?" I asked.

"Walls!" boomed the voice furiously. "Wooden walls. Walls that are made of wood!"

Maxi had climbed up and now he was smashing his paw against the statue. There was a creak followed by a clang. Maxi pulled a panel off and it revealed a rope ladder, leading into the guts of the ancient statue.

Beckoning towards Furia and I to follow, he sprang up the ladder. I climbed up behind Maxi. Torchlight bounced off the green insides of the bronze statue. It was completely hollow.

"The wooden balls?" I asked.

"Walls!" snapped the voice. "Stars of Olympuss! How many times do I have to tell you!"

Maxi raced to the spot where the sound was coming from.

"Look!" he said. "It's that old plank of wood I found on the beach. It's talking again."

"Plank?" roared the voice furiously. "Who are you calling a plank? I'm the beam of Affleana!"

"The what?" I asked.

"The Magic Beam of Affleana," gasped Maxi. "Can it be true?"

"Can what be true? I sighed. "Can't someone give me a straight answer instead of a cryptic one?"

Maxi looked towards me, his tail flicking with excitement.

"The legend says that the goddess Affleana gave Sprayson a magical talking beam to take with him on his ship, *The Pawgo*. He put the beam at the front of the ship. It had magical powers and it warned him whenever danger was near. It even helped him to find The Golden Fleas."

"Thanks for making that clear Maxi," I said. "Even I can follow that."

"But the Beam of Affleana was six

tails long and it was beautifully carved," said Maxi. "I wonder what happened to it?"

"That is a sad story. It is too long to tell," sighed the magic beam.

"But you found The Golden Fleas," I said. "Didn't your story have a happy ending?"

"Happy ending?" spat the beam, letting out a sad laugh. "The milk went sour when Sprayson married Medea. The great hero went mad. He ended up living alone on the beach. He slept under the rotten wreck of his famous ship. The hero died alone and forgotten. I was the only one left who remembered him."

Silence fell like a curtain. Finally, Furia spoke.

"That's what happens to heroes," she said, looking at Maxi.

"That's what happens when you marry a witch!" sighed the beam. "Our hero couldn't understand why his luck had gone bad. But Medea's magic was strong. I think she put a curse on him."

"So what happened to you?" I asked.

"The waves rolled in and the years rolled by," said the beam sadly. "In the end, the Pawgo was broken up in a storm. I was washed out to sea and lost."

"Well consider yourself found!" said Maxi with a laugh. "But how did you get inside this statue?"

"You can thank King Minos for that," said the beam.

"Well get ready for a new quest with a new hero," said Maxi.

"Maxipuss the modest?" I sighed.

Maxi ignored me and lowered his voice to a whisper.

"The three of us are on a secret mission to Mount Olympuss. We must find the missing straybos for Furia."

"What are straybos and who is Furia?" croaked the beam.

"This is Furia." I began, wondering how best to explain. "And straybos are little charms like the ones on Furia's collar. Show the beam your collar Furia..."

Furia let out an angry hiss.

Then I remembered. Furia's collar had been stolen, along with her precious straybos.

"Sorry, actually we can't show you the straybos because someone has stolen Furia's collar."

We stared at the beam seriously, until at last Maxi spoke.

"Will you join us, beam of Affleana? Will you join our quest?"

As Maxi spoke, I held my breath, not knowing what the beam would say. I was waiting for the most important answer of my life.

"Sorry," said the beam sadly. "I cannot join you."

Maxi's face sank.

"Why not?" he asked.

"Because King Minos has nailed me to this statue," said the beam. "I can't go anywhere."

Beam Us Up!

I took a closer look at the beam and I could see that she (for Oracles are always female) was right.

Maxi is the kind of cat who does not take no for an answer, even from a magical beam.

"Search this place!" commanded Maxi. "We must find tools."

We searched high and low but we could not find anything. I was about to give up when I spotted something in a corner.

"Will this do?" I asked, passing Maxi a rusty iron bar with a pointed edge.

"Don't worry beam!" said Maxi. "I will soon have you free."

The beam let out a high pitched scream that made us cover our ears.

Maxi dropped the iron bar in fright.

"What are you doing?" demanded the beam.

"Setting you free," said Maxi.

"With that rusty iron bar?" protested the beam. "I was carved from the finest tree in the sacred groves of ash. My branch was chosen by Affleana herself. I was shaped by master carvers using magical tools..."

"So?" asked Maxi.

"So I break easily," warned the beam. "Get the right tools!"

"Back in Rome we have a saying..." said Maxi. "The right tool is the tool in your paw."

He began to pry out the nails. The beam let out another terrible scream. I sank down to the floor, my paws over my ears. I thought that my head was going to explode.

"You are free!" cried Maxi triumphantly.

In his paw he held the magic beam.

"Beam of Affleana?" said Maxi.

I think he was hoping for some words of thanks. But the magic beam was suddenly as silent as the grave.

"Come on!" said Furia. "This place isn't safe. You've made enough noise to wake Hades."

Furia ran off and we followed her.

Trust To The Wooden Walls

"Which way now?" asked Maxi.

But there was still no answer from the beam. Maxi raised it above his head and was about to smash it against the wall when Furia stopped him.

"Trust to the wooden walls," said Furia. "That's what the beam told us, remember?"

But there wasn't a wooden wall in sight. The walls of the maze were made of stone. As we padded onwards, I got a strange feeling in my whiskers. A voice inside me told me that I was not alone. Furia had sensed something too. She stopped and sniffed the night air. We had just set off again when my heart sank like a brick. The noises had started again.

"Did you hear that?" hissed Maxi.

I nodded.

"Which way now?" I asked.

But Maxi was already gone, darting ahead of me into the long shadows.

"Wait!" hissed Furia. "There's danger ahead."

With three great springs she overtook Maxi and went tearing around the corner.

She'd disappeared from sight but I

heard her let out a terrible hiss that stopped Maxi in his tracks.

"Father Felinious!" I cried. "What in Paw's name are YOU doing here?"

But he could not answer. Furia had him pinned to the ground. She held him by the neck like a weasel on a rabbit.

"Let him go!"ordered Maxi.

Furia did not release her hold. One bite would break Felinious' neck and snuff out his candle.

"Furia!" I begged. "Let him explain!"

Something snapped in her and she released her hold.

"Why have you come here, thief?" she demanded.

"I came to bring you this..." croaked the Father.

"A shield?" I said, noticing the round wooden object on the ground where he had fallen.

"No!" moaned Father Felinious. "Why do you never get it right first time Son of Spartapuss?"

By the way that he was gasping for breath, I was afraid that I wouldn't get a second guess. I thought Furia had choked him to death. Then Felinious held up an object. It shone in the torchlight.

"Furia's collar!" gasped Maxi, almost dropping the beam in surprise.

Felinious passed the collar to Furia. The straybos shone in the torchlight.

"What's going on?" asked Maxi.

"I'm sorry," said the Father. "I should have told you from the start. Will you forgive me Furia?"

Furia held her tongue. But she didn't look as if she was in a forgiving mood.

"How did you get the collar back?" I asked.

"I liberated it from King Minos," he answered.

"You mean... you stole it back?" said Maxi. "How did you manage that?"

At that moment, a trumpet blast rang out and echoed down the passage.

"They've raised the alarm," said Maxi. "King Minos is onto us!"

"Quickly," said Felinious. "Follow me!" Furia let out an angry hiss.

"Follow you?" she spat. "Never! I will

not go a step further with you, Roman."

"Yes you will my dear," said Felinious.

Furia did not reply. She glared at Felinious as if he was a thorn that was stuck in her claw.

"Look at your collar," he said. "Count how many charms you have on it now."

Furia held up the collar. In the soft candlelight I could see that there were now three charms.

"Felinious," I gasped, "you've found another straybo."

"A little present from King Minos' collection," said Felinious.

"I still don't understand," said Maxi. "Why did you steal the collar if you were going to give it back?"

"So that I could find out where King Minos kept his treasures," said Felinious.

I looked at his eyes. There was no sign that he was lying. But some mouths pour out fresh lies like cream from the bottle.

Furia examined her collar, put it on and turned to Felinious.

"What do you know about my quest?" she asked, wide eyed in the candlelight.

"I am sorry but we must leave. There is no time to explain," said Felinious. "Follow me!"

"Wait!" I cried. "Look at this old shield. I think I've made an important..."

Felinious stopped me in mid sentence.

"The shield has a map on it," he said.

I pointed at the white pattern that was painted onto the round wooden shield. If you looked closely at it, you could see that the lines represented the passageways of the maze.

"That's exactly what I was going to say," I said.

Maxi shrugged.

"So there's a map on the shield. What are you waiting for Spartan? A round of applause?"

"Follow me!" said Felinious leading us back the way we had come. "Move quickly if you value your lives."

I had no alternative but to chase after the rest of them, sprinting like a spring hare down the passage.

We ran so fast that I thought my lungs were about to burst. Felinious seemed to have little problem keeping up with the pace. He was surprisingly quick on his feet for his age. However, Furia and Maxi got further and further ahead of us. When we turned the corner and saw the statue of the Minopaw, I begged them to stop for a moment while I caught my breath.

"Is there really a creature after us?" I asked, looking up at the statue.

Felinious laughed.

"This is your creature!" he said, pointing at the statue. "The Minopaw was a colossus – a statue, like the Terrible Tomcat of Talos."

After hearing the dreadful noises in the maze, I wasn't sure that I believed him.

"But what about the stories about the cat eating monster in the maze? There must be some truth in them."

Felinious laughed again, and ran a paw along the foot of the great statue.

"The maze is real," he said. "But the Minopaw is a statue with a hollow belly. The old King used to keep prisoners locked up inside the statue. That is where the idea of a cat eating monster came from. I'm sure that the original King Minos liked to scare his enemies (and his citizens) to death. That's how the myth of the Minopaw must have started."

I nodded, feeling a little less terrified.

"Come on Spartan," said Maxi springing to his feet. "Let's go."

As I ran after Maxi, I thought about the myth. I wondered how the poor prisoners must have felt: captured far from home, marched to a monsterous statue and forced inside to bake in the sun. I wondered what sort of twisted mind could think up a punishment like that.

I looked up at the sky – it was the colour of a poisoned well. A grey morning was arriving.

My thoughts turned to all the things I'd seen since I left home. Strays in the slave market; gladiators risking death in the arena; workers smashing rocks and mean King Minos on his golden throne. All of them lived under the same stars. Was there only one choice – to be a hammer or a nail?

I ran on. The sound of a trumpet blasted these thoughts from my mind. An unmistakeable smell drifted down the passage. Torchlight danced on the walls ahead of me. Then I heard a terrible howling noise and as I rounded the next corner, I came face to face with a real monster.

The enormous dog looked as if it had walked straight out of a nightmare. It had yellow eyes, even yellower fangs and coal black fur that stuck up like the bristles on a brush. Snail trails of drool streaked from its snarling jaws. Around its neck was a leather collar ringed by sharp spikes. It pulled forward, raking the sand with its claws. But it was held by a chain, attached to the collar. At the other end of the chain was King Minos's champion, Pantheras and twenty guards. This evil gang was grinning like a fishing crew with a full net. The hound let out a howl and to my horror its call was answered by another dog.

Twenty tail lengths in front of me, Maxi and Furia stood as still as a pair of statues at the temple gates. Neither of them moved a muscle as they faced down a second beast.

Their hound let out a deep growl. A ring of hackles stood up on its neck.

"Hounds of Hades!" said Maxi. "They're cat eaters! What now?"

"Run!" hissed Furia. "Lead the others to safety. I'll hold them off."

"Running is no use," hissed Maxi. "These beasts can run all day long. And now they have our scent."

"Pantheras,"called Felinious. "You've caught us. We surrender!"

Pantheras shook his head slowly.

"I'm sorry Romans," he said. His long tail flicked against the dusty ground. "I can't accept your surrender. I have orders from King Minos."

Pantheras reached towards the dog's spiky collar and began to untie the rope.

"Stop Pantheras!" I called. "Wait!"

But my cry was interrupted by Felinious.

"Use the beam Maxi!" he boomed.

Maxi still held the Beam of Affleana in his right paw. He brought it up as the hound of Hades came towards him. Its hot breath was steaming in the chilly air of the morning.

The hound snarled and snapped at Maxi. It was not a proper attack, just a test of his defences.

"Stop right there hound of Hades!" warned Maxi, dodging the attack.

"For Peus sake! Use the beam!' cried Felinious.

Maxi swung the beam and smashed it against the hound's leathery nose.

"Not like that!" sighed Felinious. "I mean use the magic."

Maxi's blow stopped the beast in its tracks. It had a surprised look on its face – like a bear that's just been stung by a wasp. The hound wasn't hurt, it was just amazed that a tiny creature could do it any harm.

"By The Golden Fleas!" yelled Maxi. "What shall we do now?"

"Run!'" said the voice of the beam.

There was a loud clap of thunder, and the ground under my paws began to shake. I leapt back as a section of the wall collapsed in front of me. A dark cloud of dust rose through the air.

"What happened?" I asked.

Without waiting for an answer, I span round and took off down the passage like Purrcury, (the messenger of the gods) on a next day delivery.

"Hey Maxi!" I cried. "I thought you said that running away was no use!"

"Got any other ideas?" asked Maxi.

"Let's get back to the Minopaw statue," said Furia. "We can hide inside."

It wasn't a great plan but it was all we had. Felinious checked the shield map and soon we were running back towards the heart of the maze.

A few minutes later the four of us were standing in front of the statue of the Minopaw, gasping for breath.

"What's the plan!" I moaned.

"Easy Spartan!" said Maxi. "Those guards are wearing heavy armour. We've got a few minutes to think.

I looked up at the statue, the bronze metal had turned a weird green colour. The gold tips of the creature's cruel horns gleamed in the light of dawn.

"Get it open!" said Maxi, pointing at the hatch in the statue's belly. Furia sprang up the statue's leg and clawed at the hatchway. The hatch swung open. Furia climbed inside and seconds later she let down the rope ladder. One by one we began to climb inside. Maxi went first, helping Felinious to climb up.

"Hold the ladder Felinious," said Maxi. "Furia and I will try to wake the beam."

It was my turn to climb up. Just as I put my paw on the ladder I heard the dreadful howling again.

"Faster Spartan!" called Maxi. "They're right behind us!"

As I sprang up the ladder it began to swing wildly. Suddenly I fell like a brick down a well. The next thing I felt was the rope ladder landing on top of me.

"I'm sorry," cried Felinious. "I couldn't hold it. It must have slipped though my paws."

I stared up at the open hatch. It was too far up for me to leap. I tried throwing the ladder up for Maxi to catch, but I missed.

"What can I do?" I cried in horror. The terrible howling got louder and louder.

"I'm sorry!" moaned Felinious. "But don't just stand there. You'll give us away. Find another hiding place."

I backed away from the statue, not knowing whether to hide or run.

"Close the hatch Maxi! Quickly, before they discover us," ordered Felinious.

"Stay where you are Spartan," cried Furia. "You worm!!" she hissed at Felinious. "You dropped the ladder on purpose. You want to use the Spartan to lead them away from us."

"No!" cried Felinious. "That's not true. I swear."

I didn't know if Felinious was telling the truth. I looked up. It was too high for me to leap without the ladder.

"He's right," I said. "There's no need for all of us to die here."

I picked up the fallen rope ladder and dumped it in the shadows behind the leg of the statue. Then I turned back to look up at the place where my friends were hiding.

The next thing I said was stupid, but it was also surprisingly brave.

"Close the hatch Maxi," I called. "I will lead them as far away as I can."

"No!" said Furia.

"Wait Spartan!" said Maxi. "Catch!"

"Don't call me Spartan," I moaned.

Something came flying through the air towards me. Instinctively, I stepped to the left and caught the wooden beam.

"Wait Son of Spartapuss!" whispered the magic beam. "Before I join a quest, I like to see if the heroes are true to their word. You are ready to give up your life for your friends. That reminds me of someone I used to know."

The old wood was warm in my shaking paw. I was too shocked to answer.

"There's no need to run," whispered the beam. "Walk into the shadows and watch me."

As the beam said these words, the first monstrous dog came charging around the corner. It was followed by Pantheras and the royal guards, all gasping for breath in their heavy bronze armour.

"Seal the room!" ordered the King's champion. "We have them trapped!"

Six guards rushed towards each exit. A forest of spears stood between me and every way out of the chamber.

The dog let out an excited yowl and began to sniff the air. To my horror, it came straight towards the pile of stones where I was hiding. I held my breath, wishing that I could dig a hole and bury myself but the floor here was made of solid stone. I could feel the heavy breath of the dog. Foul steam rose into the cold air. I could see the slobber running down its yellow fangs. It came closer and closer, but then it stopped.

"Hold me up," whispered the beam. Slowly, I raised the beam into the air.

The first thing I heard was a ticking noise, like the sort of sound that a kettle makes when you take it off the fire, only much much louder. This was followed by the grinding crunch of metal scraping against stone.

The monstrous dog turned its ugly head away from me, its stubby nose twitching in surprise.

"Hold me up higher," whispered the beam. "I need to see what I'm doing."

The grinding noise began again. In the light of the torches, I could see what was happening. The Minopaw was lifting up its enormous leg, the green bronze was flexing, the metal was bending at the knee. Green dust sparkled in the air, glowing like fireflies. With a thundering crash the Minopaw's great bronze foot stomped towards the dog. The hound of Hades let out a frightened yelp and dodged out of the way. Then the Minopaw began to move towards its enemy in a shower of green sparks.

The room was a cauldron of confusion. King Minos' guards were wailing in horror. Their dogs barked and howled and snarled wildly.

"Don't just stand there like kittens! Shoot it!" cried Pantheras.

He grabbed a bow from the frightened guard who stood next to him. Slotting an iron tipped arrow into the bow, he pulled back his arm. The bowstring twanged and the arrow hissed towards its target. The arrow struck the Minopaw right between its eyes, which were flaming like white hot coals. I heard the guards gasp as the arrow bounced harmlessly off the mighty statue.

The Minopaw turned towards Pantheras. I heard the ticking sound again followed by a grinding noise as its face twisted into a mask of rage.

"Kill it!" cried Pantheras, "What are you waiting for? Shoot it!"

He let loose a second iron-tipped arrow followed by another and another. But the arrows clanged off the statue's bronze skin without even leaving a mark.

"Stand and fight!" roared Pantheras. But his guards were already throwing down their weapons and running.

There was a metallic clank as the Minopaw lowered its great head. The gold tips of its horns swivelled and pointed towards Pantheras. Puffs of steam seemed to rise from its nose. Its bronze hooves made the ground shake.

"Help! It's going to charge," yelled a terrified voice. I raised the beam high in the air again. The terrified guards fled the chamber and ran for their lives. Their evil dogs chased after them with their stumpy tails between their legs.

As silence returned and the red dust settled, I held the magic beam up in the air in celebration.

"Maxi! Furia!" I cried. "You can come out. We've done it! We've won!"

Maxi was the first to come out.

"Hey Spartan!" he laughed. "I hate to admit it, but I'm impressed!"

Trust to the Wooden Walls

I am running out of space in this scroll, and so I cannot now tell you the full story of how we left that miserable island. But believe me, escaping is a lot easier when you have a magical beam on your side. Using the shield map that Felinious had stolen, we made it back to our ship and slipped away like frogs into a pond.

"It was nice of King Minos to repair *The Pawgo*," said Maxi. "I'd love to see his ugly face when he finds out that we've stolen our ship back."

I felt the ship creak and groan. The wind puffed out the sail as we sped away.

"Something has been puzzling me," I said. "The magic beam told us to 'trust to the wooden walls'. But that cryptic clue never came true."

Felinious let out a loud sigh.

"Trust to the wooden walls?" he laughed. "Is that what it said?"

"Yes," I replied. "But there are no wooden walls in the maze of the Minopaw, it was made of stone."

Felinious laughed.

"Look around you Son of Spartapuss." he said. "The answer to the riddle is under your nose."

I looked from left to right, flicking my tail against the deck. I thought and thought, but I didn't know what he meant.

"Trust to this ship," said Felinious with a sweep of his paw. "Ships have wooden walls."

Maxi and I nodded.

"It's the same advice that the Oracle gave to the city of Cathens when they were fighting the Purrsian Empire – 'trust to the wooden walls'. It meant 'get into your ships and leave!'"

Maxi let out a laugh and eventually I joined in. But one of us wasn't laughing.

"I don't trust you Felinious," said Furia.

Felinious looked into her firey eyes.

"You see plans and shadows everywhere," he said. "But you're wrong about me Furia. Who arranged to hire this ship without a captain or a crew? Who steered you through dangerous waters to an island where a straybo was hidden? Who picked two friends to help you on your quest? You might find it hard to believe Furia, but nobody wants you to succeed more than I do."

The wooden walls creaked again. Many of the planks were new. They were still expanding and slotting into their older neighbours. I saw Furia's expression change as we were carried up on the next wave. The sea was colour of dirty silver under the grey sky, but Furia was brighter.

"Where next?" she asked. Her tail had stopped flicking and her eyes were no longer on fire. She touched her collar with her paw. The three straybos caught the light of the sun.

"To Mount Olympuss of course," said Felinious. "On that famous mountain your friends may find glory at the Games."

He looked Maxi in the eye. Then he turned to Furia again, "And you my dear," he purred, "you will find the answers that you seek."

✳ ✳

Find out what happens next in:

The Olympuss Games BOOK IV

STARS OF OLYMPUSS

ISBN: 9781906132842